TUTANKHAMUN'S ARROW

Collins
RED
Storybook

TUTANKHAMUN'S ARROW

by KAREN WALLACE
illustrated by Chris Fisher

Collins
An imprint of HarperCollinsPublishers

First published in Great Britain by Collins 1998

Collins is an imprint of HarperCollins*Publishers* Ltd,
77-85 Fulham Palace Road,
Hammersmith, London W6 8JB

The HarperCollins website address is
www.**fire**and**water**.com

3 5 7 9 11 10 8 6 4

ISBN 0 00 675361-2

Printed and bound in Great Britain by
Caledonian International Book Manufacturing Ltd,
Glasgow, G64

For Rob Maddock

Chapter One

Two minutes before the end of the last
period on Friday afternoon, Mr Murdock,
the history teacher, picked up a thick
black pen and unrolled a scroll of paper.
On it he drew something like a beetle
balancing a ball on top of three
matchsticks and a
pudding bowl. It
looked like this:

Underneath, he
wrote the word
TUTANKHAMUN
in big letters.

One minute before the end of the last

period on Friday afternoon, Mr Murdock
turned to the forty faces watching him.

"Who knows anything about
Tutankhamun?" he asked.

Class 5a thought as one. With barely
thirty seconds left, any serious reply was
out of the question.

Ten seconds ticked by.

"He was a bit of a mummy's boy,"
shouted Darren Jackson from the back.

The class erupted in laughter.

Mr Murdock grinned. "Not exactly, Darren," he said. "Tutankhamun was an Ancient Egyptian king, who was preserved as a mummy and buried in a tomb beneath a pyramid." He pointed to his strange drawing. "These symbols mean Tutankhamun."

Mr Murdock pinned the scroll of paper to the wall. "Tutankhamun is going to be our new project on Monday morning," he said. "I hope everyone has a good weekend."

There was a ragged chorus of "Thank you, Mr Murdock" and "You too, Mr Murdock" as chairs scraped across the floor.

Lucy Turnball slung her backpack over her shoulder, put her head down and made for the door. Out of the corner of her eye she could see her friends Elly and Kate watching her curiously. On most days the three of them stayed behind for a quick gossip.

"You going?" called Elly.

Lucy nodded. "I have to meet my mum."

Mum worked nights at the local hospital so she wasn't able to come to the school very often. Lucy and her brother, Joe, usually walked home with a group of friends who lived in the same street. But today was different... Mum *was* meeting them. She was taking the children to a sneak preview of a jumble sale that was being held the next day in the local community centre.

Lucy and her mum loved poking through old stuff. And Lucy had a knack of finding special things. Once, at a car boot sale, she had found a sequinned waistcoat tucked inside an old sweater. Kate and Elly had gone half berserk with jealousy! *And* they didn't know that it had only cost twenty-five pence.

Joe hated jumble sales. He associated them with hanging around outside church halls while he waited for his mother and sister. They always took ages. As far as Joe was concerned, jumble sales were a complete waste of time.

So that morning, after breakfast, Lucy and Mum struck a deal with Joe. For the most part, it wasn't difficult to find a solution that kept everyone happy. Joe and Lucy got on reasonably well. Lucy was almost eleven and older than her brother, but there were only eighteen months between them. They were both tall, with the same unruly blonde hair and grey-green eyes. In fact many people thought they were twins – when they were younger, they used to pretend they were.

"How about this," said Mrs Turnball as

she made their lunch sandwiches. "I'll pick you up from school and then we'll have a quick look at the jumble before I go to work. It will only take twenty minutes."

"Twenty minutes!" wailed Joe. His heart sank. Twenty *hours* more like.

"And I'll play football with you when we get home," said Lucy in a reasonable voice. "We can walk home from the community centre, can't we, Mum?"

Mrs Turnball nodded. It was only a short walk and there were no busy streets.

"Who's going to make my tea?" asked Joe.

Mrs Turnball laughed. "Don't sound so grumpy, Joe! I'll leave your tea in the fridge and Granny said she'd drop by to keep you company until Dad gets home."

Lucy grinned at her mother. "We won't need company, Mum. We'll be playing *football*."

Mrs Turnball grinned back. "Then Granny can be referee."

"Or watch the telly," said Joe.

"Or watch the telly," repeated Mum, rumpling his hair.

And that had been that. The deal was agreed, and after school Joe was standing at the main gates. Lucy waved when she saw him. She felt for the warm fifty pence coin in her jacket pocket and thought gleefully of all the bargains she might find.

"Twenty minutes," said Joe. "OK?"

"I know," said Lucy. "That's what we agreed."

"Just checking," muttered Joe.

At that moment Mrs Turnball appeared. "Anyone for a bar of chocolate?"

"Yes, please!" they replied in unison.

Mrs Turnball handed out chocolate bars and they set off down the street.

"So, what happened at school today?"

"We got our new project," said Joe through a mouthful of chocolate.

"So did we," replied Lucy. "What did you get?"

"Henry VIII. What about you?"

"Tutankhamun."

"*Who*?"

Mrs Turnball pulled a face. "You remember, Joe. The Ancient Egyptian king we saw at the British Museum."

Joe shrugged. "Guess I'll find out next year."

Lucy exchanged looks with her mother and laughed. "Guess you will."

They turned right off the high street and crossed over a zebra crossing.

"It's over here," said Lucy, pointing across the street.

"I'll hang around outside," said Joe.

Lucy looked disappointed. "Come in," she said. "I'll feel guilty if you're waiting for me."

Mrs Turnball took Joe's arm and pulled him across the street. "Come on," she said kindly. "You might find a T-shirt that Gazza's mum threw out by mistake."

Joe allowed himself to be pushed into the community centre. "Twenty minutes," he said to Lucy under his breath.

A group of women were inside, emptying plastic sacks of clothes onto a table. A few others were already poking through the piles.

Darren Jackson's mum waved when she saw Mrs Turnball. "Almost everything's out," she called. "Have a good look. You too, Joe," she added quickly because Joe seemed so awkward standing by the door.

Lucy immediately started digging through the pile of clothes nearest her.

Joe went off into a dark corner and prodded a row of cardboard boxes.

Mrs Turnball took one look with a well-practised eye and decided to have a chat with Mrs Jackson instead.

Five minutes later, Lucy was half hidden in a rail of old coats. Probably going through the pockets, thought Mrs Turnball as she walked over to a beige mackintosh sprouting pink leggings. "I'm off, Lucy," she said. "Fifteen minutes, then straight home."

"OK, Mum. Bye."

"Bye," Mrs Turnball said and looked across the room. Joe was still in his dark corner. "Bye, Joe."

"Bye, Mum."

Fifteen minutes later, Lucy had found nothing and felt cross and disappointed. As she straightened up from the last plastic sack which hadn't been emptied, Joe tapped her on the shoulder.

"I know, I know," said Lucy, trying not to sound how she felt.

Joe looked embarrassed. "Ah, Lucy," he began, "have you got any money?"

Lucy stared at his red face. "I don't believe it!" she cried. "I thought you *hated* jumble sales. What have you found?"

"It's a bow and arrow," said Joe. He patted his pockets. "Thing is, it's fifty pence and—"

"It's yours," grinned Lucy. She fished into her pocket and handed him the warm silver coin.

"So what's so special about this bow and arrow?" asked Lucy as they walked home.

Joe shrugged. "It looks weird and I wanted it."

"Maybe you could put it on your wall," suggested Lucy.

"Or maybe I could shoot with it," said Joe. "We could make one of those big targets."

"I've never shot an arrow," said Lucy. While she was speaking she had the sudden feeling of something being close behind her. She turned and saw a black cat walking down the middle of the pavement.

Lucy stopped.

The cat stopped, too.

"That's funny," muttered Lucy.

"What's funny?" asked Joe.

"That cat. It seems to be following us."
Lucy looked puzzled. "Maybe it lives
around here."

"It better not
come home
with us,"
muttered Joe,
sniffing. Joe
was allergic to
animal hair,
which was why
the family
didn't have
any cats.

Now that Lucy was older she didn't mind that much. But there had been a time when she had wanted a kitten, especially a black kitten, more than anything else in the world.

The cat stared back at her, narrowing its big yellow eyes. Lucy had the strangest feeling it was reading her mind. When they turned into their street, she looked round.

The cat was still behind them.

Chapter Two

"Your tea's on the table," called old Mrs Turnball, as Joe and Lucy opened the front door. "I won't be a minute."

Lucy and Joe stuck their heads round the door and waved. Their granny was propped up watching an afternoon soap and embroidering another Swiss-scene cushion cover.

"Don't worry, Gran," said Lucy. "We're going to play football."

"That's nice, dear," replied old Mrs Turnball. Her eyes slid away from the screen for a split second. "This'll be over soon."

"I've heard that before," said Lucy, beginning to giggle.

"Shh!" grinned Joe. "See you in the kitchen. I'll get the football."

Five minutes later, Lucy was sitting in the kitchen but Joe still hadn't found his football.

"I've looked *everywhere*," he said. "Inside *and* outside."

"Eat your tea, first," said Lucy in a voice that sounded just like her mother's. "Have you looked under the bed?"

"Of course I have," said Joe.

"Did you see that cat anywhere?" asked Lucy, abruptly.

"No." Joe stared at the table and stuffed most of a hard-boiled egg into his mouth.

"Cheer up," said Lucy. "Let's try out your bow and arrow. We can use Dad's old dartboard as a target."

"OK," said Joe still chewing his egg.

While Joe hung the dartboard on the fence, Lucy picked up the bow and arrow and looked at it for the first time.

The bow was made of dark, almost black, wood with two fine decorative lines etched along its sides. There was the faintest trace of gold, as if the lines had once been painted.

As Lucy ran her fingers along the top, her thumb felt a tiny area of carving on the inside. She turned the bow over, and rubbed it with a wet finger.

"What are you looking at?" said Joe coming up beside her. He stared at the tiny picture carved in the wood. It looked like a beetle balancing a ball on top of three matchsticks and a pudding bowl.

Lucy laughed. "I don't believe it!"

"What?" said Joe. "What is it?"

"It means Tutankhamun," said Lucy. "Mr Murdock drew the same thing for us at school this afternoon." She handed the bow to her brother. "Some school kid must have made it as part of a history project."

"They did a good job, then," said Joe. "It *looks* as if it's really old."

As he spoke he fitted the arrow and tweaked the bowstring. It was springy and the arrow was a good tight fit. "It can't be that old if it works so well."

Lucy stepped back, shielded her eyes against the warm bright

sun, and watched Joe aim at the
dartboard. He pulled back the string
and fired.

There was a *ping* as the arrow shot
from the bow. Then it swerved past the
dartboard and disappeared into the
bottom of the thick laburnum hedge that
surrounded their garden.

"Rats!" cried Joe. "I thought it was
straight."

"So did I," said Lucy. She walked across the lawn and pushed aside the low branches of the hedge. "I'll get it."

Joe bent down beside her. "No, I will. I lost it."

"We'll both look for it," replied his sister. "We'll find it faster."

They crawled into the hedge.

"It's probably stuck in the fence," muttered Joe. "I'll look this way."

"It could be on the ground," said Lucy. "I'll stay here."

For a few moments, she pushed aside the bright shiny leaves and felt for the arrow on the ground. Nothing.

Then she looked up and her heart went *bang* in her chest! What she was staring at was impossible. Absolutely impossible.

In front of her was a full-height, simple plank door set in a sandstone wall. Stuck in the middle of the door was the missing arrow. The bow was leaning against the wall and the big black cat was sitting beside the bow.

She reached out and touched the bow. It was the same smooth wood she had held in her hand barely a few minutes before.

It wasn't a dream. It was real.

Lucy opened her mouth to scream but a choked gargle came out instead. "Joe!"

"Have you found it?" asked Joe. His voice seem to come from the middle of the hedge.

"Joe!" croaked Lucy again. "Here!"

Something in his sister's voice made Joe push through the low branches like a rhino. "What's the matter?" he yelled. "Have you cut yourself?"

The next moment he was beside her, staring at the door, the bow and the cat.

"What on earth is going on?" he whispered.

Lucy felt her eyes drawn to the black cat. It narrowed its big yellow eyes but didn't move.

"It's this cat," she said in a hoarse voice. "It's something to do with this cat."

Joe leant forward. As he pulled out the arrow, the door swung open and a hot blast of sandy air swirled around them.

The cat took a huge leap.

A gust of wind lifted Joe and Lucy like two leaves. The next moment, they tumbled through the door and landed on a flat roof covered in warm gritty sand.

"Lucy—" began Joe. But Lucy shook her head and stared, wild-eyed, around her. There was something familiar about where they were. But why? How? She *had* to remember.

They were standing on the roof of a house in the middle of a small town. In the far distance was a range of grey rocky mountains. Palm trees were growing in the foothills. Then the land evened out to broad green fields and stopped at the banks of a huge muddy river.

Lucy shaded her eyes from the sun. Painted boats sailed up and down the smooth brown water. Each one had a square white sail fixed on a mast like a home movie screen.

On the banks, men filled leather pouches with water. Others worked in the fields cutting thick green corn.

The air was still, and hot as an oven.

Joe grabbed Lucy by the elbow and pulled her round. "Look at this," he said in a voice that sounded as if it came from the bottom of a cave. "Where are on earth are we?"

In front of them was an arch that was carved and painted with tiny figures. Lucy stared at them, closed her eyes and stared again. There was a bird, a hand, a snake, a spear, and over the top of the arch a large, black-lined eye.

Suddenly she knew exactly where they were!

The figures were hieroglyphics. She had seen them on their visit to the British Museum.

She turned and looked once more at the mountains in the far distance. The scenery looked just like pictures she'd seen in the museum bookshop.

"Where are we?" said Joe again.

"I know it sounds daft, but I think we're in Ancient Egypt," said Lucy. She looked down at the bow in her hand and thought of the tiny carved picture. "In the time of Tutankhamun."

"Great," replied Joe. "Just great. I've got football practice tomorrow."

Lucy laughed nervously. "Mum and I were supposed to be going to a car boot sale."

"Then she'd better look for a second-hand time machine," muttered Joe.

Suddenly his whole face folded in on itself and a huge sneeze exploded in the air.

"Cats," he muttered.

Lucy looked again at the painted arch.

Sitting in the shadows was the big black cat.

Chapter Three

The black cat narrowed
its yellow eyes, turned,
and padded down a
carved stone staircase.

Neither Joe nor Lucy moved.

"Let's follow it," said Lucy.

Joe bit his lip. Everything was getting a
bit too spooky.

Lucy stepped onto the staircase. "We'll
call it research," she said as lightly as she
could manage. "It *is* my history project,
after all."

Lucy and Joe tiptoed after the cat and
came to a huge room with high painted

columns and a tiled floor. Slatted blinds covered the windows and it was cool and shady after the hot sun.

At the far end of the room was a raised platform. In the middle of the platform stood something that looked very much like a throne.

Lucy sniffed. There was a peculiar smell; the air smelt sweet, but sharp at the same time.

"It looks like someone's having a party," whispered Joe. He wrinkled his nose

and pointed.

At the other end of the room was a long table laid with plates of spicy beans and round flat loaves of bread. In the middle was a big bowl of marinated onions. On either side were mounds of fresh figs and dates, grapes and apricots.

Lucy grinned. Joe liked his food as simple as possible. Mango-flavoured yoghurt was about as exotic as he got. She took two steps towards the table, her eyes fixed on a fresh fig.

At that moment, they heard a low rumble of voices and the sound of clumping feet. One voice rose above the rest. It was deep and echoing, like the howl of a wolf. "We shall wait for a sign."

Joe felt his spine shiver and go cold. "Where can we hide?!" he cried.

They both turned and saw it at the same time.

Under the stairs was a big painted box.

All ideas of figs disappeared from Lucy's mind. The only problem was that her legs felt as if they were made of stone.

"I can't move," she whispered.

The voices grew nearer.

Joe half dragged his sister to the box and somehow they clambered in.

Just as he was shutting the lid, the
black cat jumped in with them.

"Oh, no!" whispered Joe. "*Now* what
am I going to do?"

But Lucy was concentrating too hard to
reply. To stop herself shaking, she was
trying to imagine what the people who
were coming into the room looked like.

She could hear the blinds being pulled
up and could see light through the cracks
in the box.

She thought of the pictures she had seen at the British Museum.

The men wore tunics and headdresses. The women wore lots of jewellery, painted their eyes black and dyed their nails and skin red.

Inside the box, Lucy could smell their perfume. It was a mixture of something sweet and something musky that made her eyes water.

Suddenly the room was silent.

"Pardon, Great One," said a man's low voice. "How long shall we wait?"

There was the scrape of a heavy chair.

"The ceremony cannot begin until the gods send us a sign," replied the woman with the low howling voice.

"But what of our king?" said another. He sounded sharp and insistent. "He waits to travel to the Underworld."

"The last journey of Tutankhamun will begin when the gods are ready," said the low howling voice. "We must wait for the sign."

Joe gritted his teeth in the darkness. A terrible tickling feeling was crawling up his nose. He knew what was going to happen and he knew there was absolutely nothing he could do about it.

A split second later, he sneezed.

It was the loudest most spluttery sneeze ever.

Lucy didn't know if she was shaking with fear or hysterical laughter. Whichever it was, her head felt as if it was going to explode.

"Open the box!" ordered the sharp voice.

Open the box. Open the box.

It sounded like the punch line of a really bad game show. Lucy was so nervous, she began to shake even more with suppressed laughter.

"Open the box!" repeated the voice.

That did it. Lucy burst out laughing.

Joe prodded her in the ribs. "Shut up!"

But Lucy couldn't shut up and when the lid was lifted, she was choking with laughter.

Crazy thoughts raced through Joe's mind. They would be abandoned in the desert. They would be sold into slavery. They would be executed for spying.

All because of a cat.

He looked around him.

The cat was nowhere to be seen.

The next moment the whole room began to clap and cheer. Voices shouted.

"It is a good sign!"

"Our king will be happy in his new life!"

A man in a white and scarlet headdress appeared behind them. It was almost as if he had been in the box with them.

Lucy jumped and her hand flew to her mouth.

The man's chest was bare except for a

wide flat necklace of green and gold discs.
Around his waist, he wore
a knee-length kilt
fastened with a
cat's-head clasp.

"I am Priest Iry,"
said the man.
He bowed low.
"You are our
honoured guests."

Lucy stared into
the man's face.
There was some-
thing strange about his eyes.
What was it?

She took his hand and stepped like a
film star from the painted box.

"Wow!" muttered Joe under his breath.

Over a hundred people were looking at them.

Suddenly embarrassed, Lucy brushed the sand from her cotton leggings and tried to pull her sweatshirt straight.

"You've got twigs in your hair," she hissed to Joe.

Joe looked down at his beaten-up trainers and pretended he hadn't heard. There was no way he was going to pull twigs out of his hair with a hundred pairs of Egyptian eyes watching him.

There was a short sharp clap of hands.

Everyone turned towards the raised platform where a woman was standing. Her black-lined eyes looked huge in her

long bony face. Her lips were scarlet.
Black hair woven with gold thread hung in
glossy braids to her shoulders.

"I am Hathor, High Priestess of Ra,"
she said.
"You are
the sign
we have
been
waiting
for."
The
sound of
her voice
made
the hairs
on Lucy's

body stand on end.

Priest Iry led them forward.

Joe and Lucy could hear the flap of their trainers on the tiled floor as they walked the length of the room.

"We should kneel," said Joe out of the corner of his mouth.

Behind the High Priestess, two frightened-looking men fanned the air with ostrich feathers. Their faces were tight and wary.

The priest caught Lucy's eye.

"Lie flat on the floor," whispered Lucy.

"OK," said Joe.

The floor was cold and slightly sticky but they kept their noses pressed to the tiles.

At last, the High Priestess grunted and

motioned them to rise.

As they scrambled to their feet, a hush filled the room and Lucy suddenly realized they were expected to speak.

But what should they say? And what if they got it wrong?

Iry laid his hands on their shoulders.

Words came into Lucy's head. "We are honoured to serve the God-king," she said.

"May his path to the afterlife be smooth," said Joe. He looked as surprised at himself as Lucy did.

The High Priestess leant forward and touched them both on the forehead.

"You have spoken true," she said. "You are among friends."

Lucy looked at the priest. His face didn't move, but something glittered in his yellow eyes.

That was you, thought Lucy. You put those words into our mouths.

As if a signal had been given, three shaven-headed musicians picked up their instruments and began to play. There was a harp and a flute and something that looked a little like a guitar.

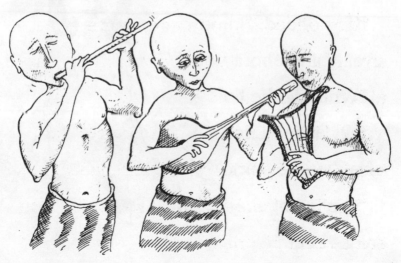

"Come," said a voice behind Lucy. "I must prepare you."

Lucy stared at a girl her own age. She had almond-shaped eyes and wore a long, white, cotton dress. Its folds were fastened by a cat's-head brooch.

"I am Kia," said the girl simply. "I serve Priest Iry. He has prepared us for your arrival."

"He has?"

Kia nodded. "I know everything about you."

"What did he tell you?" asked Lucy, afraid at the same time of what she might hear.

"You are messengers from faraway stars," Kia replied, "sent by our gods on a mission both wonderful and..."

She seemed lost for words.

Lucy stared at her. What were the words she couldn't say? Dangerous? Doomed?

"Mysterious," said Kia finally.

Lucy looked around the room. Slowly she was aware that people were leaving and the wonderful music had stopped.

A cold sweat spread across her body. Whatever their 'mysterious' mission was, everyone else seemed to know about it but them.

"Why are people leaving?" she asked, trying to keep a tremble out of her voice.

"They are going to get ready for the

procession," said Kia gently. "And so must we." She laid a light cool hand on Lucy's arm.

Lucy pulled back her arm. "What procession?"

Kia's dark brown eyes grew wide and her mouth opened in amazement. "You do not know?"

"We know nothing," said Lucy. As she spoke she felt tears pricking her eyes.

"Do not be afraid," said Kia. "You are among friends."

Lucy allowed herself to be steered to a quiet part of the room.

"Our God-king, Tutankhamun, died seventy days ago," explained Kia in a low voice. "He is prepared for his funeral procession. We have been waiting for a sign to begin the procession. You and your brother are the sign."

He is prepared.

Lucy thought of the bandaged bodies she had seen at the British Museum. "You mean, the king is a—" She couldn't bring herself to say 'mummy'. Somehow, it didn't seem respectful.

Kia nodded. "My uncle practises the noble art. He told me." She took a deep breath. "Our king's body is preserved with secret salts and herbs, then it is wrapped in

57

linen. Now it will last forever and his soul can travel to the other world."

The other world.

Lucy looked quickly around her. "Where's Joe?"

"He is being prepared," replied Kia.

"*What*?" Lucy's voice was high and panicky.

The few remaining people turned and looked at them. Kia lowered her voice to little more than a whisper. "Trust me," she said. "He is with my brother."

"Why? Where has he taken him?"

"You must understand that your own garments are not appropriate for such an occasion," said Kia matter-of-factly. "He is being bathed and dressed."

Lucy looked down at her grubby trainers and her sweatshirt. She managed a small smile. "Yes, I understand."

She followed Kia along a corridor past a group of children. Their heads were completely shaved, except for one side lock of black hair, which was carefully braided and held together with a gold clasp.

They looked so peculiar, Lucy stopped and stared.

She touched her own hair. "You're not going to—"

Kia burst out laughing. "That is the mark of a noble child. Surely you cannot think of yourself as still being a child?"

Lucy blushed. "Of course not."

She looked at the children. What did they remind her of?

"They look just like punks, don't they?"

It was the voice Lucy wanted to hear. "Joe!" she cried.

But the Joe who was standing in front of her didn't look anything like the Joe she knew. For a moment she didn't know whether to laugh or cry.

He wore a white linen kilt that came down to his knees. But his knees weren't white and knobbly anymore. His skin was dyed a deep orange.

"Bak rubbed me with coloured mud," said Joe, grinning. His teeth looked white in his suntanned face. "And he gave me this to wear. It's made from real hair!"

Joe flipped a curtain of glossy black braids across his face and did a couple of dance steps.

"What do you think?"

Before Lucy could reply, Kia pulled her firmly by the hand. "There's no time to lose," she said. "You must be made ready yourself."

Now that she had seen Joe, Lucy wasn't so worried any more. She let herself be led away.

"I'll see you later," she said to Joe. Then over her shoulder she added, "By the way, your mascara's smudged!"

Chapter Four

Joe turned when he heard the door open behind him.

"Wow!" he said. "You look amazing!"

Lucy blushed and grinned. She *was* rather pleased with her appearance.

Kia had rubbed coloured mud into her skin, too, and she had turned a deep bronze. Her black wig was longer than Joe's and some of the braids were interwoven with different coloured threads. Her lips were outlined in dark blood red, a colour her mum would never have let her wear. And she was wearing a pair of long jangling earrings which would also have been forbidden in the Turnball household.

Lucy was beginning to enjoy herself. She twirled in a circle.

"It's just like being on a movie set," she cried, as her jewellery jingled in proper Egyptian fashion.

"Sort of," replied Joe. He wasn't enjoying himself at all. While Lucy was having her Egyptian makeover done, he had had time to think.

It might *seem* like they were part of a movie set, but they weren't. They were thousands of years away from their own time with no idea of how to get home.

"Look," Joe pointed out of the window, "that's where we're going. Bak explained it all to me."

Lucy shuffled across the room in her curling silver sandals. Through the window she saw a huge crowd of people standing on the far bank of the river.

They were watching a gold boat with a blue and red sail make its way towards them.

"That boat is carrying Tutankhamun's body," said Joe. "Well, not his body exactly. It's been preserved. Bak told me. His uncle—"

"I know," interrupted Lucy. "The body's

a mummy."

Joe smiled uneasily. "I always thought a mummy was some kind of joke."

"Like time travel, you mean," said Lucy.

Heavy perfume wafted into the room. It was strong and smelt like sweet dark honey.

The High Priestess stood in the doorway. Her eyes were bigger and blacker. Her cheeks looked hollower and her lips were a slash of scarlet. She had  changed from her white robe and was now dressed entirely in gold.

"You must join the procession," she said

in her deep echoing voice. "Our king has waited long enough."

Lucy and Joe had never felt so hot and thirsty in all their lives. They had walked for what seemed like hours in the long winding procession behind the king's coffin. The sandals that had looked so gorgeous had rubbed blisters on their feet and the gold jewellery was heavy and burning-hot against their skin.

Beside them, Bak and Kia walked in silence, keeping their eyes on the huge stone funerary temple ahead.

The sound of thousands of shuffling feet and the continuous wailing of the mourners filled Lucy's head like a swarm of bees.

She closed her eyes and tried to breathe
through the cotton of her dress. The air
was choking with dust and incense.

Suddenly everything began to spin. "Joe," she croaked, "I think I'm going to—"

The next moment, she was in Bak's arms and a sharp-tasting liquid was running down her throat.

"You cannot fall," said Bak urgently. "It will be an insult to the gods."

Lucy felt a piece of sticky gum being pressed into her mouth. It tasted bitter but not unpleasant. "Chew this," said Bak. "It will revive you."

"Lucy! Lucy!" It was Joe's voice. "Are you all right?" He sounded on the verge of tears. "What did you give her?" he shouted at Bak.

"A medicine of my father's," replied Bak. "My father is a physician in the court," he added in a slightly stiffer voice.

"It's working," whispered Lucy to Joe.
"I'll be all right."

Bak took Lucy's arm and half carried
her forward. "I will help you," he said.

Joe looked at Lucy. Her eyes said leave
me, don't worry. He dropped back to
Kia's side.

In front of them, a huge triangle of
yellow stone blocked out the sky. The sun
rested on top
of it like a
decoration on
a Christmas
tree.

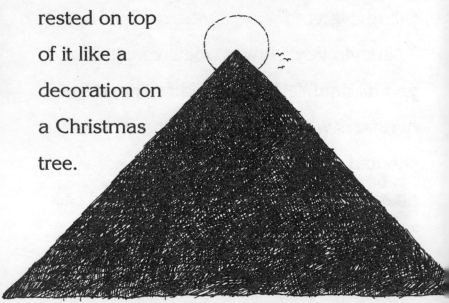

"Soon the sun will fall behind the great tomb," said Kia.

Kia was right. Half an hour later, they were walking in pale purple shadows and it was cooler. But now there was a different feeling in the funeral procession.

Everyone knew that the time for the king's final journey was almost upon them.

Joe moved up to Lucy's side. Neither of them spoke. Neither of them *could* speak. They also felt the change in the crowd and one single question loomed in their minds: *How were they going to get home?*

A wave of homesickness washed over Lucy and her eyes filled with tears.

"Don't be sad," said Bak seeing the

tears run down Lucy's cheeks. "Now the God-king will live forever and all your struggles will be over."

Joe's stomach turned to ice. "What do you mean *our* struggles?"

A terrible thought flashed through Lucy's mind. Was this the 'mysterious' part of their mission? "Are we are to be buried with him?" she almost screamed.

As Bak opened his mouth, the wailing soared to an ear-splitting scream. The procession had arrived at the funerary temple in the shadow of the great pyramid.

"Bak!" cried Joe. "You have to tell us!"

The crowd roared and rose like a huge howling whirlpool. Bak and Kia were swallowed into it.

To their horror, Joe and Lucy found themselves on their own in front of the temple, staring at the carved gold coffin of Tutankhamun.

A deep voice, like the howl of a wolf, rose from the shadows of the temple's entrance. "It is the gods' will that

Tutankhamun's bow and arrow be returned to his side."

Underneath the mud that coloured their faces, Joe and Lucy went white.

The bow and arrow!

They'd both forgotten about them.

Lucy turned to Joe shaking. "Where did we leave them?"

"In the painted box," whispered Joe.

Lucy was forcing herself to think. If the bow and arrow had brought them here, somehow the bow and arrow must be part of their journey back. If they gave up the bow and arrow, they would never get home.

"Don't say anything," hissed Lucy. "We need them."

Strong hands gripped their arms. It was Priest Iry. "I have the bow and arrow," he whispered. "I will give them to you and you will give them to the High Priestess."

Lucy felt sick as the smooth wood of the bow was pressed into her hand. "If we give her these," she croaked, "we will be stranded here forever."

"If you do not, you will die," replied Iry.

"So how can we get home?" said Joe. His voice was raw and angry. "Or do we die, anyway?"

"It is not written," said Iry.

"So what *is* written?" asked Joe rudely.

"The bow and arrow must rest with Tutankhamun," explained Iry. "He wants your happiness, not your sadness."

"But if the bow is with Tutankhamun and the tomb is sealed," cried Lucy, "how can we get back?"

"You will hide in the shadows and wait for the cat," said Iry. "Follow him. Your way home is painted in pictures."

"The cat has deserted us!" shouted Joe. "He left when—"

There was the crash of a huge cymbal.

It was an angry impatient noise.

Iry looked deep into Lucy's eyes. "Trust me," he pleaded. "See who I am. There is no more time."

Lucy stared back at his strange yellow eyes. They were *cat's* eyes.

Chapter Five

Joe looked across at the huge pyramid
that stood above Tutankhamun's tomb.
A full moon cast bright shadows on the
smooth flat stones. He and Lucy had been
hiding ever since the procession had
returned to the town.

Once the bow and arrow had been
handed over, the crowd was interested
only in the coffin. It had been easy for
Bak and Kia to lead them to a hiding
place behind a mound of stones.

Kia had given Lucy water and a basket
with their own clothes. Bak had shown
Joe a secret entrance in the side of the

tomb and taught him how to light a pottery lamp with a flint.

When Lucy questioned them, Bak and Kia could only shake their heads. They were servants of Priest Iry. They did not know why they did these things, only that the priest had instructed them to do so and they were honoured to obey.

Then they had bowed and vanished into the desert sands.

"We can't wait much longer," said Joe as more stars lit up the warm black night. "We'll look for the bow and arrow on our own."

"We'll wait for the cat," Lucy replied in a stubborn voice. "We must wait and follow it as Iry said."

"Lucy," said Joe as patiently as he could. "Why should a cat show up to lead us?"

"Don't you understand?" Lucy shouted. "Iry and the cat are the *same thing*."

Joe rolled his eyes. "Lucy—"

"Shut up!" whispered Lucy. All the dye had faded from her skin and her face and arms looked silvery in the moonlight. "Look!"

Joe looked across the sand to the smooth wall of the pyramid. A four-legged shadow, monstrously large against the flat stones, was creeping towards a lozenge-shaped hole in its side.

The cat turned, and for a split second its strange yellow eyes flashed in the moonlight. Then it disappeared into the pyramid.

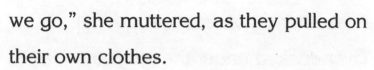

Lucy stood up. "Where the cat goes, we go," she muttered, as they pulled on their own clothes.

They followed the cat and went inside the pyramid. It was hot, and blacker than Lucy would have thought possible.

Joe struck the flint and lit the pottery lamp. Then they crawled along the tunnel towards a flickering light.

Two burning torches revealed a low-arched doorway. Joe blew out the lamp. He didn't want to use any more oil than was absolutely necessary.

"Keep your eyes peeled for the bow and arrow," he whispered.

"And the cat," said Lucy.

Joe pulled a face but didn't say anything. The last thing they needed now was another argument over the cat.

They ducked under the archway.

Lucy gasped. The room was piled high with fabulous golden ornaments and beautifully carved furniture. There were chests and chairs, and boxes inlaid with ivory and enamel. Against the wall stood a gilded wooden statue of a man holding a spear.

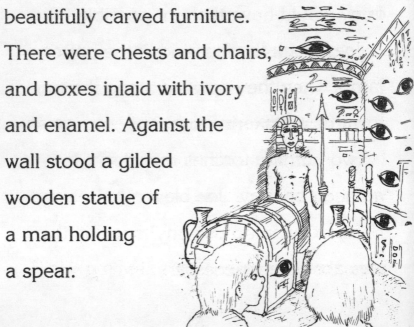

Everywhere, painted black eyes stared at them.

"Here, kitty, kitty!" called Lucy.

Her voice sounded horribly loud.

Joe took a torch and held it against the wall. "No pictures," he muttered. "Let's try another room."

The next room had money-chests lined up against the wall. There was food and drink laid out on a table. But there were still no pictures, and no sign of the cat or the bow and arrow.

In the stillness of the tomb, Lucy could hear Joe's stomach rumbling. She watched as he picked up a piece of bread.

"Don't!" she screamed, knocking the bread from his hand. "It's stealing. He'll think it's stealing."

"What are you talking about?" said Joe crossly.

"If we take *anything*, we'll never get out of here," cried Lucy. "I'm sure of it."

"Tutankhamun's dead," muttered Joe. "He can't hurt us." But he put the bread back on the table all the same.

At that moment the torches on the wall spluttered and went out.

They stood in the darkness while Joe fumbled for the flint and the pottery lamp. It seemed to take ages to get a spark. Lucy bit her hand while she waited. It was the only way to stop herself from screaming.

At last a little flame leapt up in the middle of its pool of oil. Joe shaded it with his hand. From the amount of oil, he knew they had only about two minutes left.

He looked his sister straight in the eye. "We haven't got much time."

"We have no choice," said Lucy, "we have to believe what we were told." As she spoke, she felt a sudden tingle in her left hand.

"Which way do we go?" said Joe in a hollow voice.

"What do you mean?"

Joe motioned with his hand. There was a choice of two rooms, and only enough light left to explore one.

"The left one!" cried Lucy. "Hurry!"

The little flame began to wobble.

They scrambled into the room. It was the same as the others – food, furniture, money, but no sign of the bow and arrow, and no cat.

Then in a corner half hidden behind a table, they saw him.

"The king!" cried Lucy. "We've found Tutankhamun!"

On the front of a body-shaped coffin, a huge figure stared at them with wide black-lined eyes. Its head was decorated with bands of blue and gold. Two arms were folded sternly across its chest.

It was as if the king had been waiting for them.

Joe stared at the figure's gleaming lines.

On its left sat a big black cat.

But this cat was made of shiny black wood and its strange yellow eyes were pieces of precious stone.

Joe's heart sank. If the black cat had deserted them again then...

His eyes looked down at the sandy ground. Lying there was the bow and arrow.

"Lucy," cried Joe is a choked voice. "They're here!"

"Quick," shouted Lucy. "Give me the lamp!"

She lifted the tiny flame.

Behind the cat, there were pictures on the wall. The flame wobbled.

"We must get it right," cried Lucy. "We must get it right!"

Her hand was trembling so much she could hardly see what was painted on the pictures. There was a boy and a girl. One of them was pulling back the bow. In front of them was a door with an arrow in the middle. There were other pictures...

The lamp went out.

"I've got the bow and arrow," said Joe's voice in the blackness. "What do I—"

Flickering tongues of shadow licked along the wall.

"Where are the treasure chests?" growled a man's voice. "We don't want this stuff."

There was the sound of smashed wood.

"Tomb robbers," whispered Lucy. "They'll kill us if they find us."

"I'll shoot the arrow," said Joe. "It's got to work."

Lucy could hear the taut bowstring squeak as Joe pulled it back. In her mind's eye she saw him fit the arrow just like he had in their back garden.

But there was something wrong. It shouldn't happen this way. It should...

Then she remembered. In the pictures on the wall it was a girl not a boy who had fired the arrow.

The voices grew nearer. In the growing torchlight, Lucy suddenly saw a door in the wall in front of her. It was a simple plank door just like the one in the garden hedge.

"There it is!" she shouted. "Give me the bow!"

"Where?" cried Joe. "I don't see any—"

Lucy grabbed the bow and arrow as three dark figures appeared in the door. They held torches in one hand and long curved swords in the other.

She fitted the arrow and pulled the bowstring back. It was harder than she had imagined.

The men started towards them. "Kill them!"

"Hurry, Lucy! Hurry!" screamed Joe.

The arrow sailed across the room as sword blades glinted in the torchlight.

Thwack! It hit the plank door.

Lucy threw down the bow and grabbed Joe's hand. A gust of hot sandy air swirled around them.

From far away, a roaring rattling sound grew louder and louder.

The next moment, Lucy and Joe tumbled headlong into the back garden of their own house.

Lucy lay on the grass without moving.

Over the hedge she could hear the rattling roar of their neighbour's lawnmower. Usually it drove her crazy. Now it was the sweetest sound she had ever heard.

"I don't believe it," cried Joe, pointing. "Look!"

In the middle of the garden, where no one could miss it, was the football.

Joe shook his head. "I don't understand," he began. "How—"

"We'll never know," said Lucy firmly.

"Joe! Lucy!" Old Mrs Turnball stood at the back door. "Have you finished playing football? There's a really good film on TV!"

"What about it?" said Lucy.

"Why not?"

Joe and Lucy got up and stumbled across the lawn.

"I just know you'll love it," said old Mrs Turnball. "It's called *The Curse of the Mummy's Tomb!*"

For a moment all you could hear was the roar of their neighbour's lawnmower, then Joe and Lucy fell about laughing.

Old Mrs Turnball looked puzzled. "I don't understand," she said. "Did I say something funny?"

She looked at her grandchildren rolling around on the grass, clutching their stomachs and shaking with hysterical giggles.

Old Mrs Turnball went back inside and closed the door. "Kids!" she muttered to herself. "I'll never understand 'em!"